A Night on the Range

For Dad — A.F.
For Lynne — C.S.

A Night on the Range

Aaron Frisch ~ illustrated by Chris Sheban

CREATIVE EDITIONS

Cole couldn't wait to grow up and be a cowboy.

Every day during the summer, when he always felt a strong urge to spit and walk bow-legged, Cole would mosey around wearing the cowboy boots and hat his father had given him for his seventh birthday.

His dog Bull's-Eye was his trusty mount, and the two would spend whole days out on the range. In the morning, Cole might lasso runaway horses and stubborn bulls.

In the afternoon, he'd ride the fence line and watch for rustlers. In the evening, he would put the run on hungry wolves, nipping at their tails with incredible hip shots from Quicksilver, his old six-shooter.

But it was after the sun went down that Cole wanted to be a cowboy most of all. With a day's work under his belt, he would watch black-and-white Westerns checked out from the library.

When the movies ended, he would imagine sleeping out in the wilds. It seemed to him that the very best part of being a cowboy was using beef jerky for a toothbrush, a log for a pillow, and the moon as a night-light.

One day, after watching a ball of weeds tumble along the street, Cole decided the moment had come. He sauntered over to his father, who was working on the car. Cole tipped back his hat. "I'm fixin' to become a real cowboy," he said.

"I see," said Cole's father. He wiped his hands on a rag. "What's the next step, pardner?"

"Well," Cole said, "I think it's high time I start sleepin' outside."

"Hmm," his father said, rubbing his jaw thoughtfully. "You might be right. I've heard that Buffalo Bill was sleeping outside when he was eight. The Lone Ranger, too. It's probably time."

"Yup," Cole said, hooking his thumbs into his belt loops. "I reckon so."

After a supper of baked beans and canned stew, Cole checked off his supplies.

Sleeping bag. Pillow. Bandana. Watermelon taffy.

"Well, I guess it's *adios*," Cole said to his father. He touched the brim of his hat and headed off into the sunset, Bull's-Eye at his heels.

In no time at all, Cole found the perfect camping place, between the garden and the clothesline. A cowboy always needs to be aware of his surroundings, and the spot gave him a fine view of the whole backyard. He looped Bull's-Eye's leash around a bush. He knew a cowboy was smart to keep his horse close at night.

Cole's father poked his head out the back door. "'Night, pilgrim," he said. "You want the porch light left on?"

Cole frowned. He was pretty sure cowboys' dads didn't come out to camp to say goodnight. And cowpunchers sure as tootin' didn't use porch lights. Cole squinted his eyes and nodded farewell to his father the way he thought John Wayne might. The light went out, and Cole settled in for his first night on the range.

Cole clasped his hands behind his head. The sleeping bag was soft, and the grass was cool. The stars above winked in a purple sky. A gentle breeze ruffled the leaves. All kinds of birds chirped goodnight to one another.

It was even more wonderful than Cole had dreamed. He only wished it hadn't taken him so long to do it. He figured he just might camp out every night from now on. Maybe even quit school and start learning to play campfire tunes on the harmonica.

It was going to be a splendid way to live, Cole was sure of that.

Then it got dark.

Cole never knew it could get so chilly on the range. He wondered if cowboys always got goosebumps. He didn't mind when Bull's-Eye wriggled into his sleeping bag. It didn't seem very horse-like, but it helped against the chill.

Cole wondered if cowboys' eyes always got wide when the sun went down, and if their ears were always able to hear even the smallest sounds. He pulled his bandana up and wondered at what age cowboys could tell for sure between …

crickets and rattlesnakes ...

or owls and secret calls between bandits ...

or stray cats and prowling mountain lions ...

or wind and twisters ...

or woods and grizzly bears.

Cole wondered if cowboys' legs could always move so fast at night, and if cowboys often had to carry their trusty mounts under one arm.

The next thing he knew, Cole was leaning against the inside of the back door. He took his hat off. He didn't feel much like a cowboy anymore.

Cole walked slowly into the living room. His father was reading the newspaper, and a bowl of popcorn sat on a table. "Decided to come in off the range for a bit, huh?" his father said.

Cole slumped into a chair and looked at his boots.

"I hear tell Wyatt Earp liked popcorn, too," Cole's father said.

Cole looked up and put his hat back on. Bull's-Eye came over to sniff at the bowl.

"People say he used to go riding into town in the middle of the night, past dust storms and outlaws and stampedes, just to get some 'corn. Yes sir, that Wyatt Earp was quite a cowboy."

Bull's-Eye looked at Cole and licked his chops. Cole smiled and reached for the bowl.

He thought the cowboy life just might suit him yet.